BIGFOOT
makes a
MOVIE

BIGFOOT
makes a
MOVIE

Joan Lowery Nixon

illustrated by

Syd Hoff

G.P. Putnam's Sons · New York

Text copyright © 1979 by Joan Lowery Nixon
Illustrations copyright © 1979 by Syd Hoff
All rights reserved. Published simultaneously in
Canada by Longman Canada Limited, Toronto.
PRINTED IN THE UNITED STATES OF AMERICA

Library of Congress Cataloging in Publication Data

Nixon, Joan Lowery.
Bigfoot makes a movie.
SUMMARY: Young Bigfoot's encounter with a movie-making
crew who think he is an actor in costume is very
enjoyable—for a while.
[1. Sasquatch—Fiction] I. Hoff, Sydney
II. Title.
PZ7.N65Bi   [E]   78-31106
ISBN 0-399-20684-1

With love to my son Joe

Young Bigfoot ran to his mother and father. He was so excited he could hardly grunt.

"There are lots of humans over by the highway!" he said. "They are putting a whole bunch of things in the clearing."

His father frowned. "You know we stay away
from the highway and humans."

Bigfoot remembered what happened the last time they went too close to the highway. A human saw them. And when he held a black box up to his eyes and pointed it at them, his mother and father ran back into the forest. Bigfoot was curious, but he followed his mother and father.

9

Later, Bigfoot saw something on a paper outside
the ranger station. It was blurred, but it looked like
his father. Did the man with the box do this?
Bigfoot wondered.

Bigfoot didn't understand why his parents told him to stay away from the hunters and rangers who came into the forest.

Bigfoot was lonely. And he was curious. He would like to make friends. But instead, he hid and listened to the humans. And he watched them. They had such little feet. He thought it was very funny that they didn't fall over when they walked.

Now, Bigfoot hoped he could be friends with
these other humans who had come to the clearing.
They did not look like hunters or rangers.

While his father and mother were busy building
a fire, Bigfoot hurried through the forest.

Kerblap, kerblop.

13

He was almost there when he saw another
young Bigfoot! His own size! Bigfoot was so
surprised he let out a happy roar and ran to the
other Bigfoot. He gave him a friendly hug.

But something terrible happened. The other
Bigfoot shot right out of his skin. He ran through
the forest making little squeaking sounds.

Bigfoot was disappointed. It wasn't another
Bigfoot at all. It was just a pink and shiny human,
with little feet, in what looked like a Bigfoot skin.

16

At the edge of the clearing, a girl with lots of red hair on her head hurried toward him.

"Where have you been?" she asked. "I have to run out of the trees, and you have to chase me. The publicity people from the movie studio are ready to take pictures."

She began to run toward the cliff. Rain had
made the sides of the cliff dangerous with loose
rocks. She didn't know she was in danger, but
Bigfoot knew. He couldn't tell her, so he ran after
her.

He tucked her under one arm and carried her away from the cliff to the humans who held black boxes up to their eyes.

"That wasn't the way you were supposed to do it!" she yelled. She wiggled so much that Bigfoot dropped her. The humans laughed. "Where did you learn to act?" one of them asked. Bigfoot did not like these humans.

Across the clearing Bigfoot saw some other
humans looking into strange machines. *Kerblap,
kerblop,* he went to join them. Maybe they would
like to be friends. He smiled at them.

A man in a felt hat stared at Bigfoot. "Make-up did a terrible job on you," he said. "You are supposed to look mean. The problem must be the eyebrows."

He pointed to a short, fat woman. "Go to Sadie over there, and tell her to give you heavy, mean eyebrows."

Bigfoot went over to Sadie. He smiled at her. "Awful!" she said. "Sam must have done that make-up job. The eyebrows are all wrong. Your nose is too short. And your teeth aren't big enough. Sit on this stool while I get to work."

Bigfoot sat on the stool. He let her put things on his face even though it tickled.

Finally, she said, "All right. I've done a pretty good job with your face." She handed him a flat, shiny thing.

Bigfoot looked in the shiny thing. A mean face
scowled back at him. He was so scared that he fell
backwards off the stool.

"Very funny," Sadie said. "Go over to Pete and tell him to do something with that ratty costume. You look like you're full of moth holes." She pointed at a big truck.

Bigfoot didn't know what a moth hole was. But
he picked himself up and went to the truck.

A skinny man came out and asked, "What happened to you? When I sent you out in that costume this morning, you looked pretty good." He sighed. "Well, there's nothing left to do but give it a brushing."

Bigfoot didn't like the brushing. It pulled his fur. He took the brush away from Pete and ate it.

"I'm not even going to ask how you did that trick," Pete grumbled. "All you actors think you're so funny, always showing off. Brush the costume yourself."

Someone grabbed Bigfoot's arm. "You're wanted on the set," he said. "Hurry up! The director is
waiting for you."

He pulled Bigfoot toward the humans by the machines. The man in the felt hat looked at Bigfoot carefully. "I guess you'll do," he said. "We'll be filming you from a distance anyway."

Bigfoot was so excited he couldn't make a
sound. Everyone was looking at him. They must
want to be his friends!

Then someone pushed him to a spot in the middle of the clearing. The girl with the red hair was waiting near the cliff.

35

Bigfoot wanted to tell her to get away from the cliff, but he didn't have a chance. The man in the felt hat began shouting things. The girl screamed and began to run up the foot of the cliff.

Bigfoot roared at her, but she didn't stop. She kept screaming and climbing.

Kerblap, kerblop.
Bigfoot ran across the clearing, trying to get to
the girl before it was too late.

There was a rumbling sound near the top of the
cliff. Little rocks began to slide down. Big rocks
followed them. The girl grabbed onto a small tree.
She kept screaming.

Bigfoot caught the big rocks. He threw them out
of the way, grabbed the girl and carried her down.
He ran back to the clearing and put her on her feet.

She fell over. Bigfoot picked her up again.

"That was great!" the man in the felt hat shouted.

"What's going on?" a voice yelled from the trees. It was the shiny, pink human who had jumped out of the Bigfoot skin. He was carrying the skin over his arm. "Who is that playing my part?" he asked. "I'm Bigfoot! I'm the star!"

The man in the felt hat looked at Bigfoot. He
looked at the shiny, pink human. He looked back
at Bigfoot.

43

Bigfoot roared loudly. He wanted to explain who he was. Then he smiled at his new friends. But no one smiled back. They were all staring at him.

They began running around and shouting. The girl ran faster than Bigfoot had ever seen a human run. Soon they were all in their cars and trucks, racing down the highway.

Bigfoot sighed. Those humans were not very friendly, after all. He was beginning to understand why his mother and father stayed away from humans.

He pulled off the furry eyebrows and the large nose and the big teeth and threw them on the ground. Then he saw the man's felt hat on the ground. He picked it up and put it on. He would tell his mother and father about all the funny things the humans did. He would make them laugh.

Bigfoot smiled. He would keep on trying. Someday he would meet some humans who would want to be friends.